The Colt No Man Would Ride

Joey

Ride

Linda Bailey

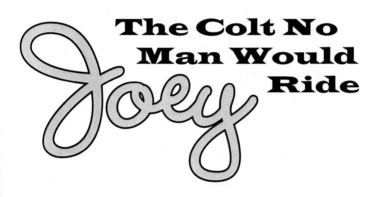

The Colt No Man Would Ride

Joey

by Linda Bailey

TATE PUBLISHING & Enterprises

Published by Tate Publishing & Enterprises, LLC
127 E. Trade Center Terrace | Mustang, Oklahoma 73064 USA
1.888.361.9473 | www.tatepublishing.com

Tate Publishing is committed to excellence in the publishing industry. The company reflects the philosophy established by the founders, based on Psalm 68:11,
"The Lord gave the word and great was the company of those who published it."

Book design copyright © 2008 by Tate Publishing, LLC. All rights reserved.
Cover design by Nathan Harmony
Interior design by Steven Jeffrey
Illustration by Jonathan Lindsey

Published in the United States of America

ISBN: 978-1-60462-512-7
1. Youth & Children: Bible Storybook (Ages 8–12)
2. Juvenile Fiction: Religious-Christian
08.01.23

Dedication

To Mark, my wonderful husband, who
believed and knew, even before I hoped to
dream, that this story would become a
book someday.

Table of Contents

Rebecca's Story

Joey's mother looked down at her little colt with love in her eyes. Most donkeys stopped having babies by the time they were twenty, but Rebecca, at age thirty-two, knew she had received her baby for a special purpose: He would do something great someday. She was reminded of another time, a time long ago when she was just about Joey's age. She had witnessed the birth of a human child born in a stable; she would never forget that night. She thought her son was very special, yet she knew he could not compare to that baby. No one could. Was that baby the reason she had Joey at her age?

"Mama, Mama."

Suddenly, Rebecca was back in the stall she shared with her son in the stable.

"Yes, son?" she said.

"Mama, what were you thinking about? I called and called and you didn't hear me."

"Oh, Joey, I was thinking of a time when I saw another very special baby born."

"Am I special?" Joey asked.

"Oh yes," Rebecca said laughingly.

"Was the other baby a donkey colt like me?" asked Joey.

"No," replied Rebecca, "this baby was human, and I just knew He was a special baby."

"How can a human be special?" asked Joey. "They only have two legs and grow up to be mean like our master."

"Oh no, Joey, not all humans are bad. This baby was very special."

"Tell me about it, Mama. Tell me abut the time you saw a human baby born."

"I was born in a stable in a little town called Bethlehem. Just a few days after my birth, we heard many people wandering about the streets of our town. I nuzzled closer to my mother, knowing she would keep me safe. She told me everything would be all right; soon everyone would go indoors to sleep. Then things would quiet down. The other animals were scared, and that frightened me. My mother tried to get me to sleep, but I couldn't. Suddenly, our stable doors opened and in walked our master. He owned the building next door that the humans called an 'inn,' a place where people sleep when they are away from their homes. It was very full because of all the people in town. Our master did a very strange thing. He brought a man and woman in to sleep with us. When I looked at the woman, she smiled at me and the other animals. We all knew we had nothing to worry about and everyone quieted down. Even the streets seemed quieter. Our master was sorry, but a stall in the stable was the best he could do. The woman smiled and said it would be fine, so our master went back inside the inn. When he was gone, the man tried to make the woman comfortable. He called her Mary, and she called him Joseph. No matter what Joseph did, Mary could not get comfortable, for she was about to have a baby.

None of us knew why, but this was going to be a very important baby.

"It didn't take long before the baby boy arrived. They named Him Jesus. They wrapped him tightly in strips of cloth. Joseph lay Jesus in a manger that we animals ate from. I wanted to look in that manger, but I was so small that the other animals crowed me out.

We heard singing coming from the hills where the shepherds were feeding their sheep. All the other animals moved to see what was happening, so I took my chance to see the baby. I leaned in to have a look; Baby Jesus looked up at me. I will never forget what I felt when He looked at me. I could feel joy, warmth, kindness, and love all at once. I will never forget those eyes. Just one look and I knew he was a great child, a king.

"A king, Mama, but how could you tell? He was just a baby, and He was born in a stable."

Rebecca wished she could help him understand how she felt when she looked into that manger that night.

"That's enough for one night. It's time you

were asleep. Maybe you will understand when you're a little older. Good night, son."

"Good night, Mama. I love you."

The Mean Master

Over the next year Rebecca enjoyed watching her little colt grow. Joey loved his mother very much and brought her much joy, but Joey hated their master who was a mean, cruel man. Joey's hatred made Rebecca very sad. She would try to tell him that she didn't feel their master was all that bad. Perhaps if he could have been in the manger the night Baby Jesus had been born, if he could have witnessed His birth the way she had, things might be different for him. Joey didn't want to hurt his mother, but sometimes he just couldn't help it. Knowing how much this hurt her, Joey decided not to talk about the baby again.

One day their master and his men came out to the barnyard and said, "Get Rebecca ready.

It's been long enough since she had that colt; she should be ready to take me to town by now." Joey knew the master was a very big and heavy man. He knew his mother was not very strong. Ruthy the goat once told him, "She never seemed to get all her strength back after having you. It's not your fault; she was just too old to have her first colt." Joey watched the men lead his mother out of the stall and saddle her. Then he saw the large master climb into the saddle. Joey could see his mother stumble under the weight. The master beat her with a whip and told her to get going. Joey, wanting to stop him from hurting her, tried to break out of the stall. Finally, the master got off his mother's back and said, "Rebecca is just too old; after having that colt, she is just no good anymore. Put the saddle on the colt. It's time he started earning his keep around here."

Joey could not believe the master thought his mother was no good and that it was his fault. He decided at that moment that he wouldn't let his master or any other man ride him. Opening the stall, the men led Joey out, but as soon as they tried to put the saddle on his back, he he kicked and jumped. He knocked one of the men to the ground. every time someone tried to saddle him he would start kicking and jumping again. They beat him with the whip, but Joey didn't care; all he knew was that no man would ride on his back. At last the master said, "That's enough, I'll take the colt to town and will sell him, You two take Rebecca over to Simon's. He said he would buy her for his children. He won't give me much, but at least I will be rid of her. I'll be rid of both of them."

Joey could not believe: They were going to take him away from his mother, He hated his master, but loved his home and the other animals. He didn't want to leave them or his mother. Joey ran to her. "Did you hear what they said? They want to take us away, away from home, away from each other!"

Rebecca looked at Joey sadly, "Yes, dear, I heard. I have known in my heart this day would come. They took me from my mother when I was about your age, and then they brought me here. I'll never be sorry because if they hadn't brought me here, I wouldn't have had you. It's your time to go out into the world. I always believed you would do something great some-day. I will miss you, but please don't worry about me. I know the Simons. They are kind and gentle people with small children who will not be too heavy for me to carry. I will be all right. But you, my little colt, you must put away your pride; you are a work animal and must act like one. I don't want anything to happen to you."

At that moment the master came to take Joey away. Joey saw him coming and he nuzzled his mother, "I will always love you, Mama," he said, and he was led away to town. The master never let him look back. If he had, Joey would have seen the tears in his mother's eyes as she watched him leave, and he would have heard her say, "I will always love you, my son. Please be good."

Joey Meets Jesus

Arriving in town, Joey and the master came to a tavern; his master decided to go in for a drink. He left Joey outside alone. *Maybe no one will want me, then my master will have to take me home. Maybe Mama is still there and I will get to see her one more time,* Joey thought.

While he was thinking, two men walked up and started to untie him. Joey became frightened. He thought, *No, you didn't talk to my master. You didn't give him any money; you didn't buy me from him. Leave me alone. I want to go home.*

As they were untying him, Joey saw his master coming out of the tavern. "Why are you untying my colt?"[1] he asked.

They said, "The Lord has need of him,"[2] and they took him away.

Joey did not understand why his master didn't try to stop them, or why they were taking him farther away from his home. *They'll see. No man will ever ride me. I'll make them want to take me home*, Joey thought. Not knowing what the men wanted, Joey was afraid.

His fears seemed to fade away, however, when they finally reached their destination. Many people were standing around, but Joey only saw one man. He was walking toward Joey, looking right at him.

"Hello, Joey," He said with the kindest voice Joey had ever heard. Joey looked into His eyes, and he felt love, joy, warmth, and kindness all at the same time. He knew in an instant; this was the one his Mama had told him about so many times. Only Mama knew Him as a baby, Baby Jesus. This was Jesus, the King.

Jesus spoke to Joey as if He had known him all his life. "Don't worry about your mother, Joey. She is in a good home with people who will take care of her. I need you now. I need you to carry Me through town. Do you think you could do that?" Joey knew he could. It would be an honor to carry this Man, this King. Soon everyone began laying their coats on Joey. Jesus climbed on his back and they started to town; Joey was proud and happy to have Jesus on his back, the back that no other man had ever ridden.

Joey Does Something Great

Simon couldn't have been happier to buy Rebecca from his neighbor. He knew Rebecca to be a kind, gentle donkey that he could trust to carry his two young children. The children were very excited to have their own donkey and wanted to go for a ride right away. Simon, being a loving father, let them ride to town with him as he went for his weekly walk. As they came into Jerusalem, he noticed a crowd had gathered at the road. They were all yelling and were excited. As Simon drew closer, he could hear what the crowds were yelling. "Blessed is the king who comes in the name of the Lord!"[3]

Simon led Rebecca and the two children to the front of the crowd so they could see what everyone was yelling about.

Rebecca could not believe her eyes. The first thing she saw was her son, Joey, with a man on his back. *He said he would never carry any man on his back*, she thought. She looked up at the man he was carrying. She took one look into the eyes of the man and she knew who He was and why her son would allow Him on his back. Joey must have known also. Those were the same eyes she had looked into at the stable all those years before. Those were the eyes of Baby Jesus, only now He had grown into a man. He truly was a king, and He was riding triumphantly into town on the back of her son. Rebecca stared up at Jesus, and for one instant she saw Jesus look down at her and smile. The same feelings she had as a young colt washed over her again. From that moment on she no longer worried about Joey. She knew he was doing what she had known he would do all along. He was doing something great; carrying the King of kings. Rebecca knew why Joey was born. She knew why she had been given a baby so late in life.

As tears of joy filled Rebecca's eyes. Simon said, "Come on, Rebecca. Let's take the children home." She was more than happy to do so. That was her job now, to care for those two little children. Joey would be okay.

Jesus' Triumph and Betrayal

Joey continued down the road with Jesus. Many people laid their coats on the ground in front of them and rejoiced and shouted, "Praise God for the mighty works He has done."[4] Joey enjoyed hearing the people, but there were some men who were not happy. They stepped up to Jesus and told Him to quiet the people down. Jesus smiled and said that if He told the people to quiet down, "then the rocks would cry out."[5] Joey thought he'd like to see that. It would not surprise him if the rocks cried out. He wanted to cry out himself. Jesus rode him up to the temple, a place where people went to pray, teach, and learn. Joey had to stay outside while everyone else went in, but; he would wait there until Jesus came out. While he waited, he saw the same men go into the temple that wanted the people to quiet down. Suddenly, Joey could hear shouting and something crashed to the ground. People and animals ran out in all directions. A little while later, Jesus came out; he looked a little angry, but Joey was not afraid of his Master. Jesus was not angry with him and would not hurt him.

Jesus let Joey take Him to Mountain Olivet, where He would go at night to rest. In the morning Joey brought Him back to the temple to teach. He did this for the next few days. Those were the happiest days Joey had ever known. Just being near Jesus was all Joey could hope for. For almost a week he watched the people come to Jesus to be taught. Great crowds would sit and listen to Jesus. Even the men who did not like Jesus always seemed to be around when He was teaching in the temple. Sometimes Jesus would be alone with His twelve friends. They would sit and eat and learn from Him. Joey thought it would be wonderful to be one of them.

After about six days, Jesus sent two of His friends, Peter and John, to town. He told them to prepare a room for a very special supper for the twelve of them. He even had a name for the supper; it was called the Passover. That night Joey followed the men into town. He watched as they entered the building with the special room. He could see a light in the upstairs window, and all the men were seated around a long table. Jesus held up some bread and broke it; He then handed it to all His friends. Next Jesus held up some wine and passed it all around. Oh, how Joey wanted to be there and hear what Jesus had to say to them. Suddenly, Judas, one of the twelve, came running out. He did not look happy. Joey wondered why he would leave. Joey waited for the Master Jesus to come out. Perhaps He would like to ride back to Mount Olivet. When Jesus finally did come out, Joey could tell that He wanted to walk. The eleven friends who were at the supper after Judas left walked with Him, and Joey followed after them. When they reached Mount Olivet, Jesus told His friends to pray, and He walked on a little farther and knelt down to pray by Himself. Joey watched from a distance. He could tell Jesus was upset and tired. He wanted

to go and comfort Him, but he felt he had better not. Whatever it was that Jesus was praying about was very important. Joey looked toward the others, and when he looked back he was surprised to see a man clothed in bright, shiny white clothes standing over Jesus. The man reached down and touched Jesus, and with that touch, Jesus seemed to get stronger. As He became stronger, He prayed even harder. He prayed so hard that He began to sweat, and

"His sweat was like great drops of blood falling on the ground."[6] Joey was frightened. He ran back to the men who were supposed to be praying for Jesus, but he found them asleep.

Joey started to wake them up, but as he did he heard Jesus' voice. "Why are you asleep?"[7] He told them they needed to wake up and pray, but even before He was finished speaking Joey saw a great crowd of men coming toward them—the men who were angry with Jesus. They brought solders with them. Then Joey saw Judas, the man who had run from the supper earlier. Judas walked up to Jesus and kissed Him.

"Judas, are you betraying me with a kiss?"[8] Jesus asked. Joey felt his own anger rise up. The rest of Jesus' friends felt the same way because they started to fight with the solders. One of Jesus' friends took out his sword and chopped off the ear of one of the soldiers. That is when Jesus said stop. He reached down and picked up the ear and put it back on the man.

"Have you come out against a robber with swords and clubs? When I was with you daily in the temple you did not try and take me."[9]

The soldiers grabbed Jesus and took Him away; all of Jesus' friends ran and hid. Peter and Joey followed at a distance. The soldiers took Jesus into a courtyard, when Joey tried to follow through the gate, the guards made him stay outside. The guard shut the gate. Joey had never felt so alone.

Peter Weeps,
Jesus Crucified

Joey was left outside the gate and could not see what was happening to Jesus. He saw Peter go inside and was glad that Jesus would have one of his friends close by. He waited all night, hoping that Jesus would come out to him and say, "Come on, Joey. Let's go home." And when He did, Joey would be there to give Him that ride.

Hours went by; Joey knew it was just about morning because he heard a rooster crow. Suddenly, Peter ran out of the gate "crying bitterly."[10] That really frightened Joey.

What are they doing to Him in there? he wondered. Soon the sun came up and the crowd come out leading Jesus to another part of town. They pushed and shoved Him. Joey saw that His face had been beaten and was badly bruised, and part of his beard had been pulled out. Jesus was led into another house, so Joey had to wait outside again. He heard a lot of shouting. This went on throughout the day. Wherever they took Jesus, Joey would follow. Finally, they took Him for a second time to a man named Pontius Pilate. It was then that Joey thought they might let Jesus go, but instead they let a bad man named Barabbas out of jail. Joey could not believe it. He watched Barabbas walk away, laughing, while Jesus stood tied and beaten as the people yelled and called Him names. They also yelled, "Crucify Him!"[11] Joey wasn't sure what that meant, but he knew it wasn't good. Suddenly, the crowd led Jesus away. Joey could see He was very weak and tired.

If only they would let me carry Him, he thought. Joey saw them strap a heavy cross on Jesus. He saw Jesus stumble, and a solder whip Him. It made Joey remember his mother stumbling under the weight of the heavy master and how the cruel men beat her.

"Let me carry it for Him," Joey wanted to yell, but no one could understand him. Joey tried to get close enough to help Jesus, but the crowd just pushed him back. That is when he saw him. He knew the man. It was Simon, the one who had bought his mother from the master. The soldiers grabbed Simon and made him carry the heavy cross, but they were still making Jesus walk up the hill. When they finally reached the top, Joey hoped it was over, but it only got worse. Joey saw them nail Jesus to the cross and put a sign over His head that read, "This is the King of the Jews."[12] Next they stood the cross between two other crosses with men nailed to them. Joey felt helpless. He could not believe how cruel the people were being to Jesus. He knew people were mean, but this went beyond what he had ever imagined. Then he heard Jesus say something he could not believe.

Jesus said, "Father, forgive them, for they do not know what they do."[13] Joey could not be sure of what he had heard. It was so noisy, maybe he had misunderstood. But Joey knew he had heard right. Still the people were yelling and laughing at Jesus. One of the men on the two crosses made fun of Jesus and laughed at Him. The man on the other cross told the cruel man to stop. Joey could not hear what they were saying, but when the one who seemed to be sorry spoke, the other stopped laughing. Jesus smiled at the man and then He said something to him. The sorry man looked at Jesus and smiled too, but he had tears running down his face. Joey could tell that the man had said, "Thank you."

Joey stood as close as he could to Jesus for about six hours. There were many people there, so he could not get too close, but he wouldn't leave. Suddenly, the sky turned dark and the ground trembled. It was frightening, but Joey would not leave. After about three more hours, the sky became light again when it did, Joey had no trouble hearing Jesus cry out, "Father, into Your hands I commit My Spirit."[14] And then Joey saw Him die.

Joey thought his own heart would break. He didn't know what to do. Then he saw her. It was Mary, Jesus' mother. She was standing at a distance, watching. She looked so tired and weak. Joey went to her so she could lean on him. She was crying and was trembling. Joey stood close so he could warm her. He knew he would take her wherever she needed to go.

Sometime later men came to take Jesus off the cross. They took His body to a tomb. Joey carried Mary behind them. Later he took her to John's house to rest. He was one of the twelve friends of Jesus. Joey stayed outside John's house all the next day just in case she needed him. But on the first day of the week,

Joey knew he had to go to the tomb where they had laid Jesus to rest. He got up early and walked to the tomb. When he arrived, he saw some women there. He looked toward the tomb and was surprised to see that the giant rock the soldiers had rolled in front of the tomb had been moved. Joey saw the women go inside. He crept up to the door and looked inside. He saw two very shiny men talking to the women, but Jesus was gone. Joey heard the men ask, "Why do you seek the living among the dead? He is not here, He has risen."[15] Joey started to back away. He heard the men say something more, but he was not sure what. He wanted to get back to Mary in case she needed him.

Jesus, Joey, and Mama

Joey rushed back to town. He wondered what the shiny men meant when they asked the women, "Why do you seek the living among the dead?"[16] Could Jesus be alive? No, Joey saw Him die on the cross. He was very confused. At that moment Joey saw two of Jesus' friends running into town. He followed them down the street and saw them head into an old building. Joey ran up to one of the windows and peered in. What he saw surprised him so much that he nearly stumbled. There in the room of that old building stood the eleven friends, and before them stood Jesus. He was showing them His hands, feet, and side. Then He sat down and began to eat and talk with them. Joey could not take his eyes off

Jesus; at one moment he even thought he saw Jesus look up and smile at him. Soon Jesus had finished eating and He led the others outside. Joey saw them start down the road, so he followed them. Jesus led them as far as Bethany, a little town nearby. Many others followed after the twelve. Jesus stopped and turned to look at every one of them; He blessed them. As Jesus blessed them, Joey and the others saw Him lifted up into the sky. No one could take their eyes off Him. Suddenly, He was gone. Joey stood there, gazing up at the sky. He no longer felt sad. In fact, he was very happy.

When he could finally tear his eyes away, he looked around at the crowd, and then he saw her. She was standing next to Simon, the man who had carried Jesus' cross up the hill.

As Joey looked at his Mama, he saw tears running from her eyes. She turned and looked at him. "Oh, Joey," she said. "I was so proud of you when you carried Jesus through town."

"But why are you crying, Mama?" Joey asked.

"Because I am so happy," she replied. "Do you know that besides one other human, I am the only being here who got to see Jesus come into this world and leave this world to ascend into Heaven?"

"What person?" Joey asked.

"Over there, son," Rebecca replied. Joey looked and saw Mary, Jesus' mother. Joey looked back at his own mother.

"Oh, Mama," he said as he sighed.

"It's okay, son. I have always known that you would belong to someone else someday. I could not be prouder than for her to own you. I know she will be kind to you for me.

She knows what it's like when your son has to leave."

Joey nuzzled his mother. "I will always love you, Mama."

"I will always love you too, son."

And at that moment they looked toward Mary and she smiled at them, and they both knew that everything would be all right.

Endnotes

1	Luke 19:33	9	Luke 22:52–53
2	Luke 19:34	10	Luke 22:62
3	Luke 19:38	11	Luke 23:21
4	Luke 19:37	12	Luke 23:38
5	Luke 19:40	13	Luke 23 34
6	Luke 22:44	14	Luke 23:46
7	Luke 22:46	15	Luke 24:5
8	Luke 22:48	16	Luke 25:5